Hope Larson • Jackie Ball • Noah Hayes • Sarah Stern

GOLDIE VANCE™

Volume Three

BOOM! BOX™

GOLDIE

BOOM! BOX™

GOLDIE VANCE Volume Three, November 2017. Published by BOOM! Box, a division of Boom Entertainment, Inc. Goldie Vance is

BOOM! Studios, 5670 Wilshire Boulevard, Suite 450, Los Angeles, CA 90036-5679. Printed in China. First Printing.

ISBN: 978-1-68415-053-3, eISBN: 978-1-61398-730-8

created by **Hope Larson** & **Brittney Williams**

written by
Hope Larson & Jackie Ball
illustrated by
Noah Hayes
colors by
Sarah Stern
letters by
Jim Campbell

cover by
Brittney Williams

designers
Jillian Crab & Chelsea Roberts
assistant editor
Sophie Philips-Roberts
editors
Dafna Pleban & Shannon Watters

chapter

NINE

issue nine cover by **Kat Leyh**

DEEP END DINER, ST. PASCAL, 9:08 PM.
DEEP END
YOU DIDN'T.
I COULDN'T HELP IT! IT WAS HILARIOUS.
I GOTTA GO, CUTIE. TELL ME THE REST TOMORROW?
JUST TRY AND STOP ME!
VROOOOOOM

SCREEEEECH
OOOF!
SLAM
bounce
CRRRUNCH

Eeeeeehhhheehhhhhh...

FLASH, IT'S A GOOD THING I WAS WEARING MY HELMET, OR MY HEAD WOULD BE SHAPED DIFFERENT...

BIG BLUE!

Oh, NO...

HEY! KID!

YOU OKAY?
I...I THINK SO.
BUT WE SHOULD EXCHANGE INFO JUST IN--

SLAM
HEY! WHAT DO YOU THINK YOU'RE DOING?!

VVRRRRROOOOM
GET BACK HERE, YOU MOOK!

HEY!

Unbelievable. Society crumbling around my ears; teens run off the road like **animals...**
UGH!
GOLDIE! WHAT HAPPENED?!
Eh?

ARE YOU HURT?
I'M FINE. NOT A SCRATCH-- SEE?

BUT BIG BLUE IS TOTALED.

WELL, BETTER BLUE THAN YOU.

AND THE ASPHALT EATER WHO RAN ME OFF THE ROAD TOOK OFF WITHOUT EVEN OFFERING ME A RIDE.

WHY, I-- mmph!
THANK HEAVENS YOU GOT YOUR MOTHER'S HARD HEAD...
hug!

WHAT AM I S'POSED TO DO NOW?
I THOUGHT THIS YEAR I'D HAVE ENOUGH SAVED FOR A CAR FROM HERMIT'S USED, BUT NOW I'VE GOTTA BLOW EVERYTHING ON A NEW BIKE.

REMEMBER THAT GAME, *CHUTES & LADDERS?*

I ALWAYS HATED THAT ONE. IT DOESN'T TAKE ANY SKILL AT ALL, JUST DUMB **LUCK.**

THAT'S THE GAME. THEY SHOULD'VE CALLED ***THAT*** GAME *"LIFE".*

I AM SORRY TO HEAR ABOUT YOUR BIKE, THOUGH, SUNSHINE--BUT HEY, I'VE GOT SOME GOOD NEWS!

A WATER MAIN BURST OVER AT THE PINK STAR CASINO, SO *PRESCRIPTION ONE* BOOKED THEIR DRIVERS INTO THE CROSSED PALMS FOR THIS WEEKEND'S RACE!

I KNOW HOW MUCH YOU LOVE GETTING A CHANCE TO DRIVE THOSE NICE CARS.
THEY WON'T LET ME PARK THE ***RACE CARS,*** DAD. BUT THANKS FOR TRYING TO CHEER ME UP.

THE NEXT DAY...
...I MEAN, HE MEANT WELL, BUT I DON'T GET MY GRITS WATCHING SPOILED RICH KIDS DRIVE CARS THEIR PARENTS GAVE THEM.
THAT'S NOT ALL THEIR PARENTS GAVE THEM...
LOOK AT THOSE CHEEK-BONES.
LOOK WHO'S WITH THEM.
OF COURSE SUGAR MAPLE'S GOT HER CLAWS IN PRESCRIPTION ONE.
CATCH YOU LATER, CHER. I'M TOO HACKED OFF TO FIGHT WITH HER HIGHNESS TODAY.

THE VALET STAND.
I KNOW SUGAR'S NOT YOUR FAVORITE, BUT HOO BOY CAN SHE DRIVE!
THANKS, ROB. YOU KNOW JUST WHAT TO SAY.

SHE'S BEEN TEARING UP THE RACETRACK ALL SEASON.

SHE WAS ONE OF THE FAVORITES TO TAKE THE CUP, BUT NOW THAT LEWIS IS OUT, SHE'S A SHOO-IN!

SPEAK OF THE DEVIL...

...AND SHE SHALL APPEAR.
SUGAR. HELLO.

YOU'RE ON BREAK NOW. SCRAM.

YOU'RE NOT OUR SUPERVISOR, YOU--
STOW IT, GOLDIE. I'M NOT HERE TO ARGUE.

I NEED YOUR HELP.

WH... WHAT?
YOU KNOW MORE ABOUT CARS THAN ANYONE ELSE IN THIS SINKHOLE OF A TOWN-- AFTER ME, THAT IS.

EXCUSE ME, BUT I HAVE WORK TO DO. MOST OF US DON'T GET PAID TO LOLLYGAG, AND YOU HAVE ALL THE HELP YOU NEED.

DON'T GET FROSTED, GOLDIE. I HEARD YOU'RE HAVING SOME TRANSPORTATION ISSUES.
HELP ME OUT, AND I'LL LET YOU PICK OUT WHATEVER YOU WANT FROM HERMIT'S USED CAR LOT.

WHAT SEEMS TO BE THE TROUBLE, MISS MAPLE?

I THINK BETTER ON THE ROAD. LET'S GO FOR A DRIVE.

YOU DON'T HAFTA TELL ME TWICE! I'D RIDE THIS CAR TO MERCURY.

I THINK SOMEONE'S TRYING TO SABOTAGE ME.
ALL RIGHT, SUGAR, WHAT GIVES? MUST BE THE END TIMES IF YOU'RE ASKING FOR MY HELP.

MY *P1* CAR'S BEEN ACTING... FUNNY. I ***KNOW*** THAT CAR. SOMEONE'S BEEN TAMPERING WITH IT, I'M SURE OF IT.

IT'S A POOR CRAFTSWOMAN THAT BLAMES HER TOOLS, SHUG. SURE *P1* ISN'T MORE THAN YOU CAN HANDLE?

REALLY, *"DEE?"* MORE THAN I CAN HANDLE?!

I'LL ***SHOW*** YOU WHAT I CAN HANDLE.

HONK
HONK
Huh?

WHOA! SUGAR?! AND-- THAT'S HER! THE MYSTERY RACER!*
*See Goldie Vance issue #1!
VRRRRRM-VRRRRRRRRRMMMM
AND THEY WANNA RACE?! Oh, MAN! THE GUYS ARE NEVER GONNA BELIEVE THIS.
Ping

SCREEEEEECH

VRRRRRRMM
block
VRRRRRRRRRMM
SCREEEEECH

WHOOOO!
ALL RIGHT, SUGAR, I'LL HEAR YOU OUT!
BUT ONLY 'CAUSE I RESPECT YOU AS A DRIVER--NOT 'CAUSE I DON'T THINK YOU'RE A SHE-BEAST.
FINE.
WHAT MAKES YOU THINK SOMEONE'S AFTER YOU?
"USUALLY I RACE WITH SNOWBALLS, 'CAUSE, WELL, THEY LOOK BOSS."
"NATCH. WHO DOESN'T LOVE WHITE-WALL TIRES?"
"BUT LAST WEEK, THAT GROADY WEASEL LEWIS STOLE THEM. HE TOOK THE WHEELS RIGHT OFF MY RIDE, THE NIGHT BEFORE THE RACE.
"NO ONE BELIEVED ME. LEWIS COVERED HIS TRACKS. HE HAD A RECEIPT FOR WHITEWALLS, BUT I'M SURE HE TOOK MINE JUST TO GET IN MY HEAD."

"SO YOU WANT ME TO PROVE LEWIS IS SABOTAGING YOU?"
"THAT'S JUST IT. AT THE END OF THE RACE, LEWIS CRASHED. MANGLED HIS WHOLE CHASSIS."
THEY SAID IT WAS HIS ENGINE, BUT I KNOW I SAW THAT WHITEWALL BLOW OUT.
SO SOMEBODY SABOTAGED YOUR TIRES BEFORE LEWIS DID.
EXACTLY. SOMEONE'S TARGETING ME, AND IT'S SOMEONE WITH ACCESS TO MY CAR.
RIIIIIING

WHAT THE HECK?! THAT ALMOST SOUNDS LIKE--

RIIIIING

A PHONE. HOW DOES SHE HAVE A PHONE IN HER CAR?

RED! HI! ARE YOU COMING? I GOT YOU BOX SEATS AND--
bump
Oh... OKAY. NO, I UNDERSTAND. I--
SHATTER

BLAM
LOOK OUT!
-GASP-
SCRREEEEEEEEECH

R-RED? GOTTA GO. I HIT SOMETHING.

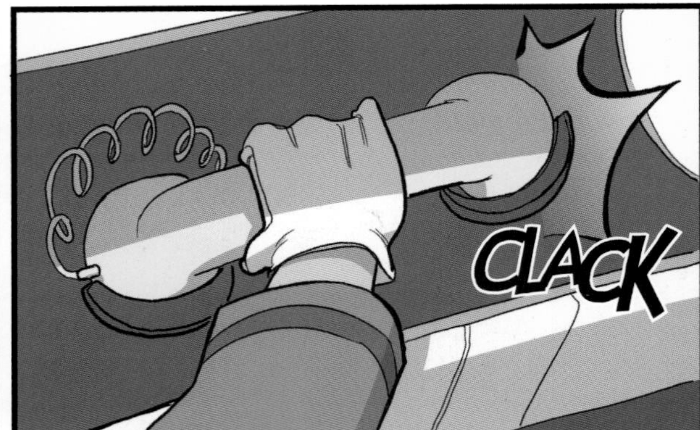
CLACK

ARGH! I CAN'T BELIEVE THIS! IF I HADN'T BEEN ON THE CRUMMY PHONE, I WOULD'VE SEEN THAT STINKING BOTTLE!
8
SAY, WHO'S "RED"? A NEW BOYFRIEND? YOU'RE GONNA BREAK SKUNK'S HEART!
SHUT YOUR FACE, GOLDIE. SKUNK IS NOT MY BOYFRIEND. AND NEITHER IS RED--SHE'S MY SISTER.

YOU HAVE A SISTER?! I THOUGHT YOU WERE AN ONLY CHILD!
YOU NEVER MET HER. SHE'S OLDER.

I WAS ON TRAINING WHEELS WHEN SHE GOT MARRIED AND MOVED OUT TO TEXAS.
AND NOW SHE HAS KIDS, AND FLORIDA AND TEXAS AREN'T EXACTLY NEIGHBORS...

BUT SPEAKING OF BOYFRIENDS--MY EX, LAZLO, IS A P1 RACER.
HE FELL OUT OF HIS TREE WHEN I DUMPED HIM LAST MONTH. HE'S GOT PLENTY OF REASONS TO WANT ME TO LOSE.

IS THERE ANYONE ELSE WHO MIGHT HAVE IT OUT FOR YOU?
HAHA. THE LIST OF PEOPLE WHO DON'T IS WAY SHORTER. I KNOW WHAT PEOPLE THINK OF ME.

"BUT IT'S DIFFERENT WHEN I'M ON THE TRACK.
8
11

"OUT THERE, THEY ALL LOVE ME."

BUT NOW I CAN'T EVEN TRUST MY OWN CREW.
HOW CAN I RACE WHEN I DON'T KNOW WHAT'S COOKING UNDER THE HOOD?
I DON'T APPROVE OF YOU RICH-KID DRIVERS, BUT...
...I'D GIVE MY LEFT LEG TO GET MY HANDS ON ONE OF THOSE FANCY P1 ENGINES.
I CAN GET YOUR HANDS ON ONE OF THOSE ENGINES!
Huh?

GOLDIE VANCE, YOU JUST JOINED MY PIT CREW. WELCOME TO *TEAM MAPLE!*
!!!

chapter TEN

issue ten cover by **Nneka Myers**

ST. PASCAL SPEEDWAY, 7:31AM.
I ♥ GOLDIE
YOU THE NEW GIRL?
POP
Huh?

C'MON SMALL FRY, AIN'T GOT ALL DAY.

HI! I'M GOLDIE VANCE, I'M HERE TO CHANGE TIRES.

YOU'RE LATE. I'M MINNIE, BUT DON'T CALL ME THAT.
...WHAT SHOULD I CALL YOU?

I'M THE CREW CHIEF, SO--CHIEF. BUT BETTER YET, DON'T CALL ME AT ALL. JUST DO YOUR JOB, DO IT FAST, AND DO IT WELL.

ANY QUESTIONS? *YOU* FIGURE 'EM OUT, OR YOU'RE FIRED.
Heh heh, NO PRESSURE, *huh?*

DON'T BE CUTE. NO TIME FOR CUTE. JUST CHANGE THE TIRES AND KEEP OUT OF THE WAY.
shzzzzzzz

WELCOME TO THE ***SUGAR SHACK***--NOW GET CRACKING, NEW GIRL.
Maple Leaf
8
WATCH OUT!
SORRY!
CONCH
GASOLINE
bounce
8

YOU'VE GOT ONE DAY TO GET YOUR BEARINGS, THEN YOU'RE ON THE TRACK WITH ME, AND I DO ***NOT*** LIKE REPEATING MYSELF.

SO MUCH FOR TEAM BUILDING, sheesh!
DON'T WORRY 'BOUT MINNIE.

SHE'S BRILLIANT, BUT SHE RULES WITH AN IRON FIST. LONG AS YOU DON'T DO ANYTHING TO HURT *THE LEAF* OVER HERE, SHE WON'T CLOBBER YA.
'SIDES, IT'S BETTER TO DEAL WITH HER THAN SUGAR MAPLE. THAT GAL'S A NIGHTMARE ON WHEELS.

TELL ME ABOUT IT...
BUT IT'S NICE THAT SHE ONLY HIRES GIRL MECHANICS, EVEN IF SHE IS A LIZARD-WITCH.

SURE. IF WE'RE WORKING FOR HER, WE AREN'T *COMPETING* WITH HER.
NEVER THOUGHT ABOUT IT THAT WAY. I'M MEREDITH, BY THE WAY. IF YA NEED ME, JUST HOLLER.

THESE GALS SEEM PRETTY ON THE LEVEL. I CAN'T IMAGINE ANY OF THEM DOING ANYTHING THAT MIGHT HURT A CAR...

WHAT'S THAT?

TOLUENE
DANGER
CROSSED PALMS RESORT. THIS IS CHERYL AT THE FRONT--

WHAT D'YOU KNOW ABOUT TOLUENE?

HELLO, GOLDIE. I'M NOT A CHEMICAL ENCYCLOPEDIA. I'LL LOOK IT UP FOR YOU AT THE LIBRARY AFTER MY SHIFT.
YOU'RE THE BEST, CHER! I'LL BUY MILKSHAKES AT THE DEEP END LATER!

YOU NEVER BUY THE MILK-SHAKES--
HEY! WHAT ARE YOU DOING IN HERE?!

Oh, FLASH!

EASY, NEW KID--I'M JUST YANKIN' YOUR CHAIN. YOU'RE GOLDIE, huh?

THEY CALL ME POPS. MINNIE WANTS YOU ON THE TRACK TOMORROW, SO I'M SUPPOSED TO MAKE SURE YOU CAN CHANGE A TIRE.

Pfft!

CHANGE A TIRE?! STEP ASIDE, MEREDITH, I'VE GOT MY DIGNITY TO UPHOLD!
BANG

click

clap clap
NOT BAD, NEW KID.

BUT IF YOU DON'T DROP FIVE SECONDS, MINNIE WILL DROP *YOU* OUT A SECOND STORY WINDOW.

FIVE SECONDS IS *GRAVY!*
BUT GIMME A MINUTE. MY ARMS ARE TIRED.
SAY, WHAT HAPPED WITH THAT LEWIS CAT? I HEARD HE HAD SOME KIND OF ACCIDENT?
I WASN'T IN THE PIT THAT DAY, BUT I HEARD THE EXPLOSION FROM THE GARAGE.
THEY SAY WHEN THAT TIRE BLEW, HE WAS SECONDS FROM THE FINISH LINE.

POOR GUY. HE WAS KIND OF A JERK, BUT HE DIDN'T DESERVE TO GET ***PRUNED*** LIKE THAT.

OKAY, POPS, FIRE UP THE STOPWATCH. I'M GONNA SMOKE MY TIME.
IF YA SAY SO.

click
0000
GO!
CLANG
HOLY CATS! THAT'S THE FASTEST ROOKIE CHANGE I'VE SEEN IN YEARS!
YOU *SURE* YOU'VE NEVER CREWED A RACE BEFORE?!
WHAT CAN I SAY? I DO EVERYTHING FAST.
TEAM MAPLE, FALL IN!

READY FOR INSPECTION, MISS MAPLE.
WE'LL SEE ABOUT THAT...
WHAT'S THE POINT OF PAYING FOR SNOWBALLS IF THEY LOOK LIKE THEY WERE DRIVEN BY SOME OFF-ROADING HOBO? GET THEM CLEANED.
IS THAT A CRACK IN THE TAILPIPE?! I WANT THAT PRETTY-BOY LAZLO TO KNOW EXACTLY WHO DESTROYED HIM IN THE TIME TRIALS, AND A *CRACKED TAILPIPE* SENDS THE WRONG MESSAGE.
IS IT *"THE THING"* THESE DAYS TO HAVE MESSY PAINT LINES ON WORLD-CLASS RACING CARS? IF NOT, MAY I SUGGEST A STENCIL?
UNLESS IT'S NOW COMMON PRACTICE TO LIGHT THE ENGINE *ON FIRE* AS PART OF A STANDARD TUNE-UP, GET RID OF THOSE SCORCH MARKS, AND DO A *FULL ENGINE* CHECK AFTER THIS TRIAL.
YES, MA'AM.
ALL RIGHT, LADIES, LET'S GO PRACTICE FOR PERFECTION!

St. PASCAL SPEEDWAY, MAGNOLIA CUP TIME TRIALS.
Maple Leaf
VRRRRRRMMMM
VRRRRRRMM
VRRRRRRMMMM

TIME?
YOU SHAVED .65 SECONDS OFF YOUR TRACK RECORD.
I CAN DO BETTER.
WRRRRMMMMM

NICE RUN, LAZLO, BUT YOU'RE NEVER GOING TO BEAT ME FOR THE CHAMPIONSHIP.

LATER THAT EVENING...
fwsssssssh

SO, D'YOU ONLY WORK ON FANCY P1 CARS NOW?
JUST BECAUSE YOU'RE MECHANIC TO THE RICH AND FAMOUS DOESN'T MEAN YOU'RE GONNA GO CHANGING ON ME, DOES IT?
NOT ON YOUR LIFE!
SO, I RAN INTO CHERYL. SHE ASKED ME TO BRING YOU THIS, SINCE YOU'RE TOO BUSY BEING A *HOT SHOT* TO VISIT HER.

Toluene is a type of particularly incendiary fuel often used in rocket experiments. It could be extremely dangerous, so BE CAREFUL.
-Cher

HEY DIANE, I'VE HAD ENOUGH OF ENGINE GREASE FOR THE DAY, WHADAYA SAY WE GO DIG UP SOME DIRT?

I THOUGHT YOU'D NEVER ASK!

I don't know, Goldie, are you **sure** this is your crook? He hasn't really done anything all that shady--
Oh yeah?

DO ***THEY*** LOOK LIKE THE SORTA CROWD A PREPPY BOY LIKE LAZLO USUALLY HANGS WITH?
I KNOW THOSE PUNKS! THEY TRIED TO LIFT A CRATE OF ALBUMS FROM THE STORE.
I HAD TO CHASE 'EM OUT WITH A BASEBALL BAT.
I'VE GOTTA HEAR WHAT THEY'RE SAYING...

I'LL HONK THREE TIMES IF YOU'VE GOT COMPANY.

I DON'T WANT ANYBODY GETTING *HURT,* IS THAT CLEAR?

DON'T SWEAT IT, MONEYBAGS, WE'LL DO OUR PART.

I STILL CAN'T BELIEVE YOU'RE SO HUNG UP ON SOME *PURSE* YOU WANT US TO BLOW YOUR CHANCES IN THE RACE.
WHAAAAT?!

YEAH, WELL, YOU'VE NEVER MET SUGAR MAPLE.
*LAZLO IS SABOTAGING **HIMSELF?***

SLAM

WE'VE GOTTA GET BACK TO THE TRACK!
YEAH? WHAT'S THE SCOOP?

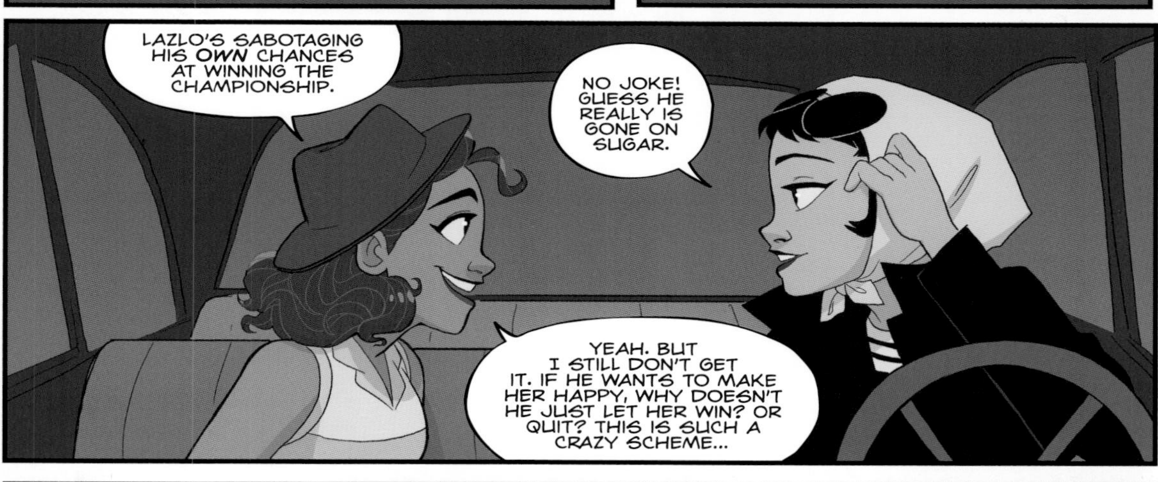
LAZLO'S SABOTAGING HIS OWN CHANCES AT WINNING THE CHAMPIONSHIP.
NO JOKE! GUESS HE REALLY IS GONE ON SUGAR.
YEAH. BUT I STILL DON'T GET IT. IF HE WANTS TO MAKE HER HAPPY, WHY DOESN'T HE JUST LET HER WIN? OR QUIT? THIS IS SUCH A CRAZY SCHEME...

I DUNNO, GOLDIE. PEOPLE DO SOME BONKERS STUFF FOR LOVE.

MR. THORPE...
WHY DID THESE NICE YOUNG LADIES INSIST ON BRINGING ME OUT TO THE TRACK, AND TELLING ME YOU'RE GUILTY OF *SABOTAGE?*

I DON'T KNOW WHAT YOU'RE GOIN' ON ABOUT.

ADMIT IT, LAZLO, YOU PAID A COUPLE OF LOWLIFES TO SABOTAGE YOUR CAR SO YOU WOULDN'T WIN THE RACE!

LOOK--
YOU DID *WHAT?*

I'M SORRY, SUGAR! I COULDN'T HELP IT! I WAS STUCK BETWEEN THE RUBBER AND THE ROAD!
IF I LET YOU WIN THE RACE YOU'D KNOW, AND YOU WOULDN'T RESPECT ME.
IF I BEAT YOU, YOU'D NEVER SPEAK TO ME AGAIN!
...
I COULDN'T TAKE THAT CHANCE, SUGAR. I'D RATHER **BLOW** OUT THAN BE WITHOUT **YOU!**
Ahem GIVEN YOUR CONFESSION, IT GOES WITHOUT SAYING THAT YOU ARE **EXTREMELY** DISQUALIFIED.
BUT ALSO IN LIGHT OF YOUR CONFESSION, I WILL ALLOW YOU TO COME TO THE RACE AS A SPECTATOR, IF MISS MAPLE THINKS IT APPROPRIATE.
THAT'S FINE, I GUESS. I MEAN... DO WHAT YOU WANT. I DON'T CARE.
COME ALONG MR. THORPE, I'LL ESCORT YOU TO YOUR VEHICLE.

BE NICE, GOLDIE. I GOTTA GO. WE GOT THE NEW ROCHELLE RAND ALBUM IN, AND I HAFTA DO INVENTORY TONIGHT.
I'M ALWAYS NICE!

SO...
SHUT UP!
I DIDN'T SAY ANYTHING!

COME ON, SUGAR, JUST HAVE AN EMOTION!

LAZLO'S GOT A FEW MARBLES TO COLLECT, BUT I BET HE'D MAKE AN OKAY BOYFRIEND.

THERE'S STILL SOMEONE OUT THERE WHO IS TRYING TO SABOTAGE ME.
I KNOW. BUT DON'T WORRY, SHUG--I'LL FIND THEM. I ALREADY CAUGHT ONE SABOTEUR, AND I'VE ONLY BEEN AT IT A DAY!

I'LL GET TO THE BOTTOM OF IT.

CHIEF! IS THE LEAF READY TO RACE TOMORROW?!

DID THAT KID REALLY SABOTAGE HIS OWN CAR?
YEP.
WOW. THAT'S SOME KINDA CRAZY.
YEAH, WELL... ANYONE WHO'S CRAZY ENOUGH TO FALL FOR SUGAR MAPLE CAN'T BE FIRING ON ALL CYLINDERS.
I THINK WE MANAGED TO GET A LITTLE MORE POWER OUT OF HER--

KNOW WHAT?

FORGET IT. I'M TAKING IT FOR ANOTHER TEST RUN.
Huh?

SUGAR, WHAT'S--
SHADE-BANS
MapleLeaf

GET OFF THE TRACK, VANCE. I DON'T NEED YOU HERE. I'M PAYING YOU TO CHANGE TIRES AND SOLVE CRIMES, AND YOU'RE NOT DOING EITHER.
WHAT?!

IF YOU WEREN'T SO BUSY PLAYING CHATTY CATHY WITH MY CREW YOU MIGHT'VE FOUND THE REAL SABOTEUR BY NOW!

AND HERE I THOUGHT YOU WERE STARTING TO GROW A HEART. MAYBE IF YOU EVER BOTHERED TO MAKE A FRIEND INSTEAD OF PAYING PEOPLE YOU CAN BE A HEEL TO, YOU WOULDN'T HAVE SOME MANIAC TRYING TO END YOUR CAREER!

WHAT THE--?
WHAT'S THAT?!
SLAM
rrrrumble
THE SABOTEUR!

NO, WAIT! SUGAR, THE CAR!
VVRRRRRRMMMM
SUGAR!
8
Maple Leaf

chapter ELEVEN

issue eleven cover by **Kassandra Heller**

DID SHE JUST DRIVE OFF THE TRACK??
IS SHE CRAZY? THAT THING'S NOT STREET LEGAL!
WE HAVE TO GET SUGAR BACK!
THERE WAS SOMETHING ON THE UNDERSIDE OF HER CAR!
NO DICE, NEW GIRL. WE CAN'T CATCH UP WITH HER. WE'LL JUST HAVE TO WAIT HER OUT.
TIRES
SHADE-BANS
I CAN'T HANDLE THIS! IT'S BEEN FORTY-FIVE MINUTES, SHE MUST HAVE WIPED OUT!
SHE'S OUT THERE IN SOME HUGE STACK UP, OR MAYBE HER CAR EXPLODED!
EASY, KID, DON'T FLIP YOUR WIG...
I DON'T BELIEVE THIS, THAT LOUSY, SABOTAGING SNAKE GOT THE DROP ON US!
I WASN'T FAST ENOUGH, AND NOW SUGAR'S BLEEDING IN A DITCH SOMEWHERE--
VRRRRRRMMMM
VRRRRRMM

SLAM
SUGAR!
GAH!
WHAT THE--?
ARE YOU OKAY?!
WHAT ARE YOU DOING YOU LUNATIC?!
WHAT'S THE MATTER WITH YOU, VANCE? ARE YOU AS CRAZY AS YOU ARE TERRIBLE AT CATCHING CRIMINALS?

Oh. SHE'S FINE.

OF COURSE I AM! WHAT'S GOT YOU IN A TWIST?
Oh, NOTHING. JUST--

--SABOTAGE!
SHOULD WE TOUCH IT?
WHAT DO YOU THINK IT IS?

IT'S A BOOSTER CONTROL! SEE, IT'S TIED INTO THE FUEL LINE HERE, AND IF YOU LOOK JUST THERE, THERE'S AN ITTY-BITTY TANK THAT STORES A KICK. JUST ENOUGH TO GIVE THE LEAF A LITTLE EXTRA OOMF!

TOSS

FLASH! SO IT'S NOT TO STOP SUGAR FROM WINNING--IT'S TO GUARANTEE SHE DOES!

DON'T LOOK AT ME LIKE THAT! *I* DIDN'T DO IT.
WHO ELSE WOULD BE CHEATING FOR YOU?
I DON'T KNOW, BUT IT WASN'T ME! GOLDIE'S KNOWN ME SINCE WE WERE KIDS--SHE KNOWS I HAVE ***PRINCIPLES.***
Ummmmm...
SO THEY'RE NOT GONNA GIVE ME ***MISS CONGENIALITY.***
I DON'T CHEAT!
Sure thing, Boss, but...
Somebody put that booster there...
NOTED. BUT FOR ***FUTURE REFERENCE,*** THESE ENHANCERS CAN BE DANGEROUS. JUST... BE CAREFUL, YOU KNOW?
TELL IT TO WHOEVER MESSED WITH MY CAR!

WHY WOULD I HIRE YOU IF I WAS SABOTAGING MYSELF?
I KNOW YOU DIDN'T DO IT. YOU MAY BE A JERK, BUT YOU'RE NO FOOL. *LAZLO*, ON THE OTHER HAND--

I DOUBT *HE'S* INVOLVED. YOU HEARD WHAT HE SAID: HE KNOWS WHAT I'D DO TO HIM IF I FOUND OUT HE CHEATED *FOR* ME.
STILL, LAZLO'S DELINQUENT BUDDIES MIGHT KNOW SOMETHING--

DON'T YOU WANT TO LOOK AT THAT DEVICE, AND SEE IF IT GIVES YOU ANY CLUES?
SUGAR, IS THERE SOME REASON YOU DON'T WANT ME TO TALK TO THOSE GUYS?
NO! I MEAN, IT JUST SEEMS LIKE A WASTE OF TIME, AND SINCE I PAY YOU BY THE *HOUR*--
SINCE WHEN IS MONEY AN OBJECT? BUT I PROMISE TO MAKE IT QUICK.
WAIT!

I... I HIRED THEM TO RUN YOU OFF THE ROAD.

YOU WHAT?!
WHAT? Y-YOU'RE FINE, AREN'T YOU? I NEEDED YOUR HELP, AND SINCE YOU'RE ALWAYS RIDING AROUND ON THAT CRUMMY BIKE I KNEW YOU'D JUMP AT THE CHANCE FOR A NEW SET OF WHEELS.
NO HARM, NO FOUL.
BESIDES, I KNOW THOSE GUYS. THEY AREN'T THE *FASTEST*, BUT THEY'RE EXPERT STREET DRIVERS. THERE'S NO *WAY* YOU'D HAVE GOT HURT.
TELL THAT TO MY HELMET! AND BY THE WAY, LITTLE MISS "*I DON'T CHEAT*," RUNNING SOMEONE OFF THE ROAD TO TRICK THEM INTO *HELPING* YOU SOUNDS LIKE CHEATING TO ME!
WELL, THAT'S DIFFERENT! THAT'S LIFE, THAT'S NOT A COMPETITION...
Life is a competition and I'm winning!

~sigh~
OKAY, YOU'RE RIGHT. I'M SORRY. BUT COME ON, GOLDIE, I KNOW YOU HATE ME. WITHOUT AN *INCENTIVE*, YOU NEVER WOULD'VE HELPED ME.
I DON'T HATE YOU, SUGAR. AND MAYBE I WOULDN'T HAVE HELPED. I DON'T KNOW. BUT YOU CAN'T *MANIPULATE* PEOPLE INTO DOING WHAT YOU WANT.
AND FOR THE RECORD, IF YOU WEREN'T SO MEAN TO ME ALL THE TIME, I PROBABLY WOULD HAVE HELPED YOU FOR FREE.
I'M NOT **MEAN.** I'M... ANTAGONISTIC.
BESIDES, IT'S NOT LIKE YOU *CARE* WHAT I THINK. YOU'RE ALWAYS SWANNING AROUND WITH THE *GOLDIE FAN CLUB.*
IS... IS SUGAR... **JEALOUS** OF ME??

I DON'T LIKE WHAT YOU DID, BUT I WON'T LEAVE YOU HANGING. ALL THAT OTHER STUFF IS IN THE PAST.
BUT IF I'M GONNA SOLVE THIS CASE, AND YOU'RE GONNA DO WHAT *I* SAY.
ONLY IF YOU PROMISE NOT TO STEAL MY CAR AGAIN...
WELL, I CAN'T PROMISE THAT, HAVE YOU *SEEN* THAT THING?
Racing
UGH. FINE. BUT I'M NOT CALLING YOU BOSS.
AND NO MORE HIRING STOOGES TO RUN ME OFF THE ROAD!
FINE, WHAT'S THE PLAN, *PARTNER?*

TOLUENE.
TOL-YOU-WHAT?
I THOUGHT THE SABOTEUR WAS USING IT TO BLOW OUT YOUR TIRES, BUT IT'S ALSO USED IN ROCKET FUEL.
IT'S AN ACCELERANT-- EXACTLY WHAT YOU'D NEED IF YOU PUT A BOOSTER ON SOMEONE'S CAR.
WHAT ARE WE WAITING FOR? LET'S FIND THE CLOD WHO'S MAKING A CHEATER OUT OF ME!
DETECTIVE LESSON #1: EVEN CRIMINALS SLEEP.

WE CAN GET AN EARLY START TOMORROW, BUT TONIGHT, I NEED FORTY WINKS AND A RIDE HOME.

THE NEXT DAY...
MARIGOLD? SWEETHEART? SUGAR WITH YOUR COFFEE?
YESSS PLEEEEASE.
WHAT? NO. SUGAR MAPLE IS HERE, WITH COFFEE.
FIFTEEN UNCOMFORTABLE MINUTES LATER...
I'M, um, SORRY FOR GETTING YOU FIRED THAT ONE TIME.
MUCH APPRECIATED, MISS MAPLE.
uggghhhhhuuugghhh...
HAVE A NICE DAY, SWEETHEART.
ssssllluuurp

SOON...
GOOOOD MOOOORNING, ST. PASCAL!
SO ANYWAY, THERE ARE THREE BUSINESSES IN ST. PASCAL THAT CARRY TOLUENE.
NEXT TIME, YOU GET DECAF.
LAB ONE...
LAB TWO...
LAB THREE...
Written out by Oceanside Bank in the name of Sarkara Estates LLC.

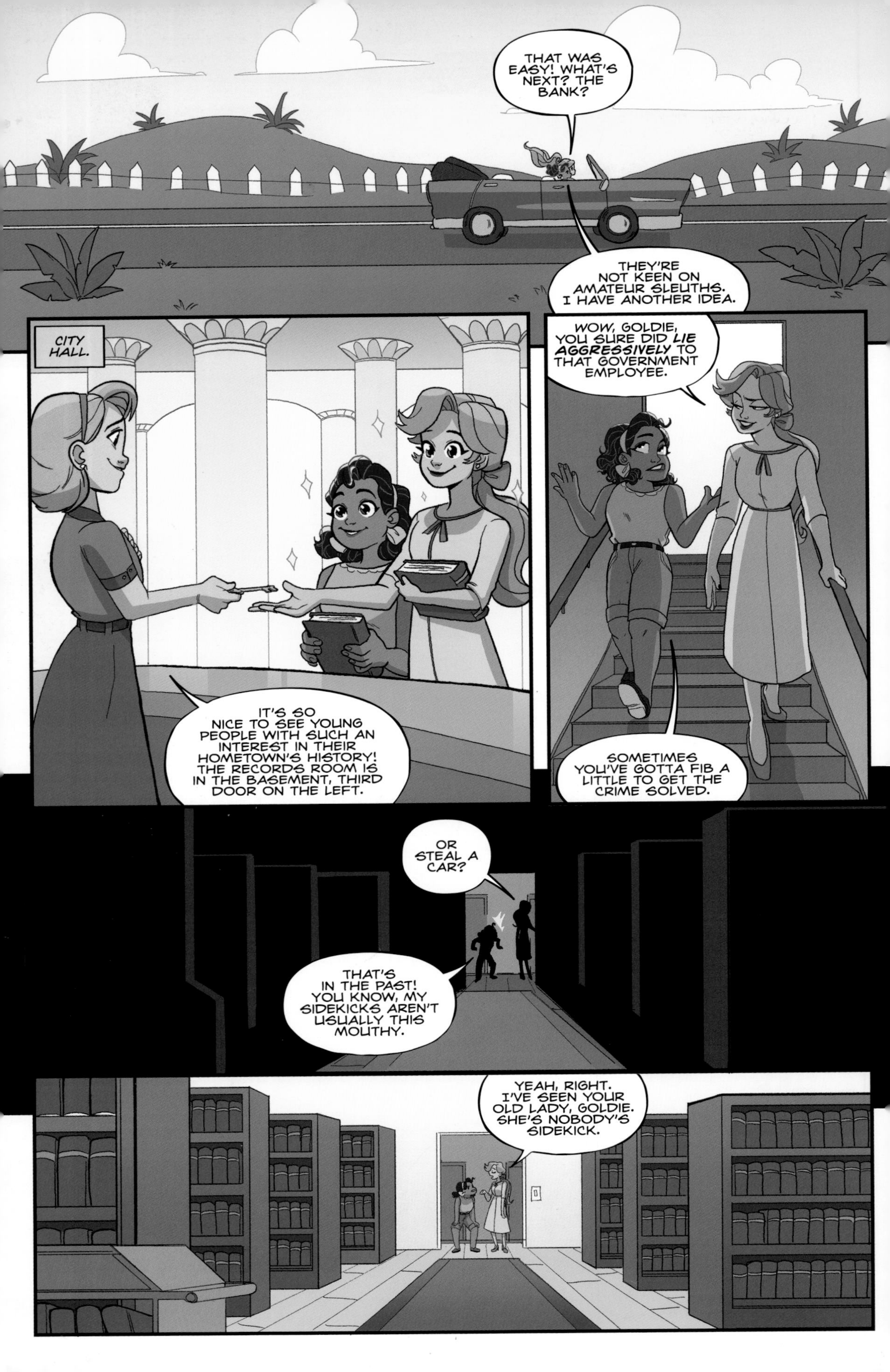
THAT WAS EASY! WHAT'S NEXT? THE BANK?
THEY'RE NOT KEEN ON AMATEUR SLEUTHS. I HAVE ANOTHER IDEA.
CITY HALL.
IT'S SO NICE TO SEE YOUNG PEOPLE WITH SUCH AN INTEREST IN THEIR HOMETOWN'S HISTORY! THE RECORDS ROOM IS IN THE BASEMENT, THIRD DOOR ON THE LEFT.
WOW, GOLDIE, YOU SURE DID LIE AGGRESSIVELY TO THAT GOVERNMENT EMPLOYEE.
SOMETIMES YOU'VE GOTTA FIB A LITTLE TO GET THE CRIME SOLVED.
OR STEAL A CAR?
THAT'S IN THE PAST! YOU KNOW, MY SIDEKICKS AREN'T USUALLY THIS MOUTHY.
YEAH, RIGHT. I'VE SEEN YOUR OLD LADY, GOLDIE. SHE'S NOBODY'S SIDEKICK.

DID YOU JUST COMPLIMENT A HUMAN BEING?

SHE WEARS LIPSTICK LIKE SHE INVENTED IT, AND SHE DOESN'T LET ANYONE TELL HER HOW TO WEAR HER HAIR. I RESPECT THAT.

...EVEN IF SHE DOES DRESS LIKE A BEATNIK.

Phew. FOR A SECOND, I THOUGHT YOU'D BEEN BODY SNATCHED...

HERE! ***SARKARA ESTATES,*** OWNED BY...

MAPLE HOLDINGS?
WHAT?!

MAPLE HOLDINGS CEO OF RECORD GARFIELD MAPLE! MY DAD?!
I GUESS HE JUST... REALLY WANTED YOU TO WIN?

I CAN'T BELIEVE THIS. I AM SO GOOD AT DRIVING. IT'S THE ONE THING I'M GREAT AT. WHY DOESN'T ANYONE BELIEVE I CAN WIN ON MY OWN POWER?
EVEN LAZLO THOUGHT HE HAD TO STOP HIMSELF FROM BEATING ME...

HOW DARE THEY?!

RIIIIIP

COME ON, GOLDIE. WE'VE GOT SOME ACCUSING TO DO!

DADDY?
SUGAR? GOLDIE? WHAT'S GOING ON HERE?

GOSH, DADDY, I WAS JUST WONDERING...

WHY YOU OWN A COMPANY THAT RECENTLY PURCHASED PERFORMANCE ENHANCING FUEL FOR P1 CARS!

YOU... YOU WERE NEVER SUPPOSED TO KNOW.
HOW COULD YOU DO THIS?! I'M NOT A CHEATER, DADDY! WHY DON'T YOU BELIEVE IN ME?!
I DID! I DO! BUT THOSE BOYS ARE SUCH GOOD DRIVERS, I COULDN'T TAKE THE CHANCE--
IT'S NOT YOUR CHANCE TO TAKE! WHY CAN'T YOU LET ME STAND ON MY OWN FOR ONCE?
IF I FAIL, IT'S NOT THE END OF THE WORLD!

BUT THAT'S JUST IT, SUGAR, IT *IS.* THE END OF MY CAREER ANYWAY. THE END OF OUR MONEY...
WHAT ARE YOU TALKING ABOUT?

I'VE BEEN HEMORRHAGING MONEY FOR YEARS. EVER SINCE YOUR SISTER LEFT, THE COMPANY'S BEEN IN THE RED, AND I'M OUT OF OPTIONS.

SO, I INVESTED IN P1. IN YOU, SUGAR. I PUT EVERYTHING ON THE LINE, AND IF YOU *LOSE...*
WE LOSE EVERYTHING.

I'M SORRY, SUGAR...

COME ON, GOLDIE, I'LL GIVE YOU A RIDE HOME.

YOU CAN STOP THE INVESTIGATION. I GUESS I DON'T HAVE ANYTHING TO PAY YOU WITH, ANYWAY.
I'M SORRY, SUGAR.
HOW WAS YOUR DAY WITH MISS MAPLE?
IT WAS... ENLIGHTENING.
I USED TO BE SO JEALOUS OF SUGAR. SHE GOT EVERYTHING SHE WANTED--ALL SHE HAD TO DO WAS SNAP HER FINGERS.
BUT, ALL THE MONEY IN THE WORLD DOESN'T MAKE UP FOR HAVING SUCH A MESSED-UP FAMILY.
MAKES YOU APPRECIATE YOUR OL' DAD, *huh*?
WELL, YEAH. I MEAN, WE'VE HAD SOME TIMES. THE DIVORCE AND ALL THAT.
BUT YOU AND MOM WERE ALWAYS THERE FOR ME.
THE MAPLES JUST... THROW EACH OTHER UNDER THE BUS AT EVERY TURN.

I FEEL SORRY FOR SUGAR.
AND ALL THINGS CONSIDERED, SHE COULD HAVE TURNED OUT... MUCH WORSE.
WHAT DO YOU MEAN?
DO YOU REMEMBER SUGAR'S BIG SISTER AT ALL?
NOPE.
SHE WAS OLDER. AND I HATE TO JUDGE A KID, BUT SHE WAS MEAN. THE WAY SHE'D TORMENT THE MAIDS AT THE HOTEL... WHO KNOWS WHAT SHE DID TO HER SISTER.
FLASH! THAT'S IT! RED MAPLE NEVER STOPPED HURTING HER FAMILY!
THANKS, DAD! GOOD TALK!

WALT! I NEED YOUR HELP ON A CASE.
GOLDIE. I HAVEN'T HEARD FROM YOU IN THREE DAYS, I THOUGHT MAYBE I'D FINALLY GOTTEN SOME PEACE AND QUIET.
NEVER!
ALL RIGHT FINE, KID. FILL ME IN.

ONE DETAILED EXPLANATION LATER...

I NEED ALL THE INFO I CAN GET ON MAPLE HOLDINGS.
SO, YOU DON'T EVEN NEED MY HELP, YOU NEED--
I NEED YOU TO CALL YOUR GIRRRRLFRIEEEEEND!
sigh
HOLD PLEASE.

I'M GLAD YOU'RE LOOKING INTO THE MAPLE FINANCES, WALT. I GOT SOME INFO ON THE BUSINESS WHEN I WAS PUTTING A FILE TOGETHER DURING THE ASTRONAUT CASE.*
IT'S ALL PRETTY SUSPICIOUS, SO I PUT A FILE TOGETHER, BUT I GOT PULLED ONTO ANOTHER CASE AND HAVEN'T BEEN ABLE TO FOLLOW UP.
*See Goldie Vance issue #5!
THE TROUBLE STARTED WHEN GARFIELD MAPLE GAVE RED, HIS ELDEST, THE KEYS TO THE GRAND MAPLE SKI LODGE.
SHE WENT BANKRUPT FASTER THAN YOU CAN SAY, "ENTITLED." DADDIO REFUSED TO BAIL HER OUT, AND BEST I CAN TELL, THEY'RE ESTRANGED.

BUT THE SKI LODGE WAS JUST THE FIRST IN A STRING OF POOR BUSINESS DECISIONS.
I DON'T HAVE ACCESS TO DETAILED FINANCIAL RECORDS, BUT IT DOESN'T TAKE A BUSINESS DEGREE TO SEE THAT THE MAPLE ESTATES IS IN TROUBLE.
gasp

SHE TANKED IT!
WHAT? WALT, IS THAT YOUR ASSISTANT?

HE'S MY ASSISTANT TODAY! AND HE JUST HELPED ME CRACK THE CASE!
ALRIGHT, BRING IT HOME, DETECTIVE VANCE.
RED TOOK IT AS A PERSONAL INSULT WHEN HER DAD DUMPED HER IN THE SNOW AT THE GRAND MAPLE. SHE BANKRUPTED THE LODGE ON PURPOSE!
AND SHE'S SABOTAGED EVERY ONE OF HER DAD'S INVESTMENTS FOR THE PAST FIVE YEARS--INCLUDING HER OWN SISTER!
The Daily TRIB
LOCAL MAGNATE LOSES SHIRT ON RISKY SKI-LODGE GAMBIT!
By Maribeth Fjørdjiensen
In a surprising turn of events, local property tycoon Garfield Maple,
normal operating accid- ents over the course of its first year have cost the company dearly.
As would be expected of him in such a sit- uation, Garfield Maple
me more than to shut the doors of one of our properties, but one unprofitable investment cannot be allowed to drag down an entire company."
"This was totally expected!" said nobody, because, as stated prev- iously, this is a very
THAT'S PRETTY SERIOUS STUFF. WE DON'T HAVE ENOUGH EVIDENCE TO BRING HER IN.
YOU WILL WHEN I CATCH HER RED HANDED!
-Groan-
ANYTHING ELSE YOU CAN TELL US ABOUT RED MAPLE?
WELL, AFTER THE LODGE FLOPPED, SHE MOVED TO TEXAS. MARRIED A RADIO MAN. THEY HAVE TWO KIDS IN EL PASO.
Oh, NO.

I JUST FOUND OUT WHO'S BEEN DOING RED MAPLE'S DIRTY WORK.
AND SHE'S BEEN UNDER MY NOSE THIS WHOLE TIME.

8

chapter
TWELVE

issue twelve cover by **Brittney Williams**

ST. PASCAL SPEEDWAY: UPSETTINGLY EARLY IN THE MORNING.
ST PASCAL SPEEDWAY
SNORT
GOLDIE VANCE: DESPERATELY SLEEP DEPRIVED TEEN DETECTIVE.

ZZZZZZZZZZZZZZZZZZZZZZ...
SUGAR, WAKE UP.
SUGAR MAPLE: SURPRISINGLY LOUD SNORER.

WHA??

I'VE BEEN AT THE POLICE STATION ALL NIGHT! THEY TOLD ME ZILCH, EXCEPT THAT POPS WON'T TALK...
IS IT BAD THAT I'M STILL HOPING YOU'RE JUST A LOUSY DETECTIVE AND YOU'RE **WRONG** ABOUT ALL THIS?
8

TO BE HONEST, I'M HOPING THAT TOO.
I'VE ALWAYS KNOWN RED IS A... PIECE OF WORK, BUT NO MATTER HOW MEAN SHE WAS TO ME, I JUST WANTED HER TO LOVE ME. I'M SO PATHETIC...

YOU'RE NOT PATHETIC, SUGAR. AND THAT'S COMING FROM YOUR WORST ENEMY, SO YOU KNOW IT MUST BE TRUE.
UNFORTUNATELY FOR YOU, I THINK THAT COVETED TITLE NOW GOES TO MY SKUZZ SISTER.

WELL IF IT MAKES YOU FEEL ANY BETTER, I SPENT THE WEEK PALLING AROUND WITH THE CRIMINAL I WAS TRYING TO CATCH, WHICH IS NOT MY MOST SHINING MOMENT AS A DETECTIVE.
Ugh... DON'T EVEN GET ME STARTED ON POPS! I CAN'T BELIEVE I'VE BEEN ***PAYING*** THAT TRASH-WEASEL TO SABOTAGE MY RIDE.

LISTEN, SUGAR... YOU DON'T HAVE TO DRIVE. WHAT IF THE TRASH-WEASEL PULLED SOMETHING BEFORE WE COTTONED ON? YOU'VE GOT NOTHING TO PROVE.
NO, GOLDIE.

BUT--
THIS ISN'T JUST ABOUT MY PRIDE. I'M NOT GONNA BE THE REASON YOU AND YOUR DAD ARE OUT OF WORK AGAIN.

ALRIGHT, FINE. BUT IF YOU'RE GOING TO DRIVE, YOU'RE NOT GOING TO DO IT ALONE--
GET OUTTA THAT ENGINE, MISS MAPLE!

I DIDN'T CALIBRATE THAT THING TO WITHIN AN INCH OF ITS LIFE JUST FOR SOME HAM-FISTED DRIVER WITH A WRENCH TO RUIN ALL MY HARD WORK!
ALLOW ME TO TRANSLATE: "WE GOT YOUR BACK, MISS MAPLE."
I MADE A FEW CALLS.
NOW LET'S FALL IN!
AND THAT MEANS: "SORRY THAT WE DIDN'T BELIEVE YOU ABOUT THE SABOTEUR."
PAT
THANK YOU ALL, FOR COMING. I KNOW IT'S NOT EASY, SINCE ONE OF THE PEOPLE ON THIS TEAM-- ONE OF THE PEOPLE WE TRUSTED--WAS WORKING AGAINST US FROM THE START.
BUT... ALL THAT'S IN THE PAST. I TRUST EVERY ONE OF YOU WITH MY LIFE. AND MORE IMPORTANTLY, WITH MY CAR.

NOW, LET'S GET TO WORK!
...WE NEED TO STOP PRETENDING...
...THERE'S NO FREE HAPPY ENDING...
...SO TAKE SOME TIME BEFORE YOU GO...
...YOU NEVER KNOW UNTIL YOU KNOW...
THANKS FOR STICKING WITH ME INTO THE WEE HOURS. THAT WAS MY NEW FAVORITE BAND: CHARLOTTE LIGHT AND THE HUMMINGBIRDS, WITH THEIR BRAND NEW SINGLE: YOU NEVER KNOW UNTIL YOU KNOW.
WE CAN'T FIND ANYTHING. NOT A BOLT IS OUT OF PLACE ON OUR GIRL, I'D STAKE MY REPUTATION ON IT.
THAT'S GREAT... BUT I'VE STILL GOT A BAD FEELING.

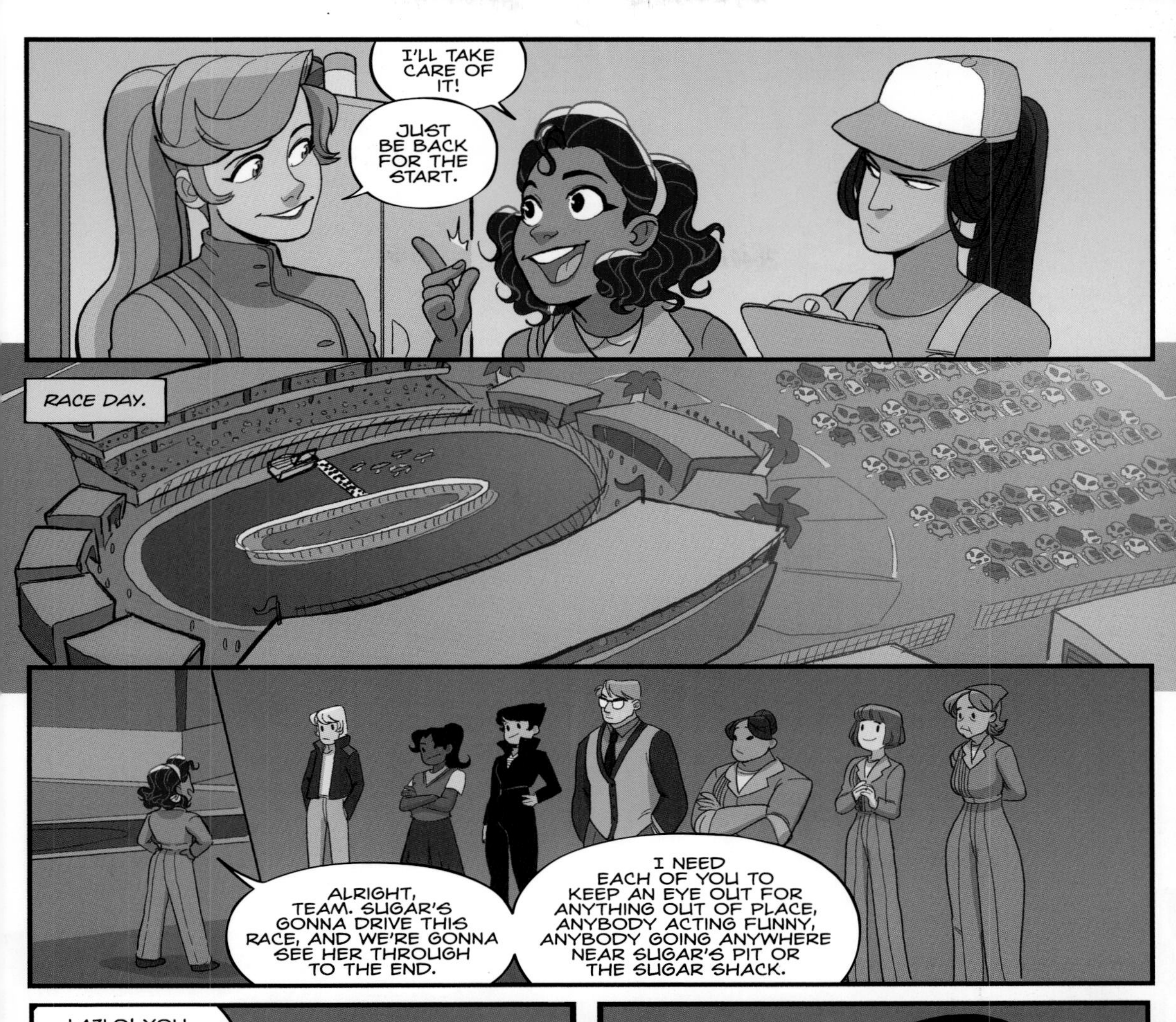
I'LL TAKE CARE OF IT!
JUST BE BACK FOR THE START.
RACE DAY.
ALRIGHT, TEAM. SUGAR'S GONNA DRIVE THIS RACE, AND WE'RE GONNA SEE HER THROUGH TO THE END.
I NEED EACH OF YOU TO KEEP AN EYE OUT FOR ANYTHING OUT OF PLACE, ANYBODY ACTING FUNNY, ANYBODY GOING ANYWHERE NEAR SUGAR'S PIT OR THE SUGAR SHACK.

LAZLO! YOU KNOW THESE PIT CREWS AND HOW THEY BEHAVE. KEEP AN EYE OUT FOR UNUSUAL FACES AND MISPLACED ITEMS.
YES, MA'AM!

CHERYL! DIANE! YOU'RE ON GROUND PATROL. LOOK FOR ANYONE WHO LOOKS LIKE YOU MIGHT HAVE TO CHASE 'EM OUT OF THE RECORD STORE WITH A BASEBALL BAT.
10-4.

ASSISTANT WALT! COURTNEY! GWEN! BONNIE! YOU'RE IN THE STANDS! KEEP YOUR EYES ON THE CROWDS FOR ANYBODY LOOKING PARTICULARLY SLEAZY, CREEPY, OR MALICIOUS!

ALRIGHT, EVERYBODY GET TO YOUR STATIONS! SUGAR'S PUTTING HERSELF ON THE LINE FOR THE CROSSED PALMS STAFF, SO LET'S MAKE SURE SHE GETS OUT OF THIS THING WITH A WIN.

ONE MINUTE TO RACE START, CREWS PLEASE CLEAR THE TRACK.
QUIT SWEATING, GOLDIE. YOU'RE GIVING ME A BAD VIBE. I'LL BE FINE. I'VE GOT YOUR CRACKERJACK SECRET SERVICE WATCHING MY BACK, DON'T I?
IN THAT CASE, GO LAY SOME RUBBER AND KICK THEIR BUTTS!
I ALWAYS DO!
RACERS, ON YOUR MARK...
BEEP
SCRRRREEEEE
"AND THEY'RE OFF!"
WWRRRRMMMMM

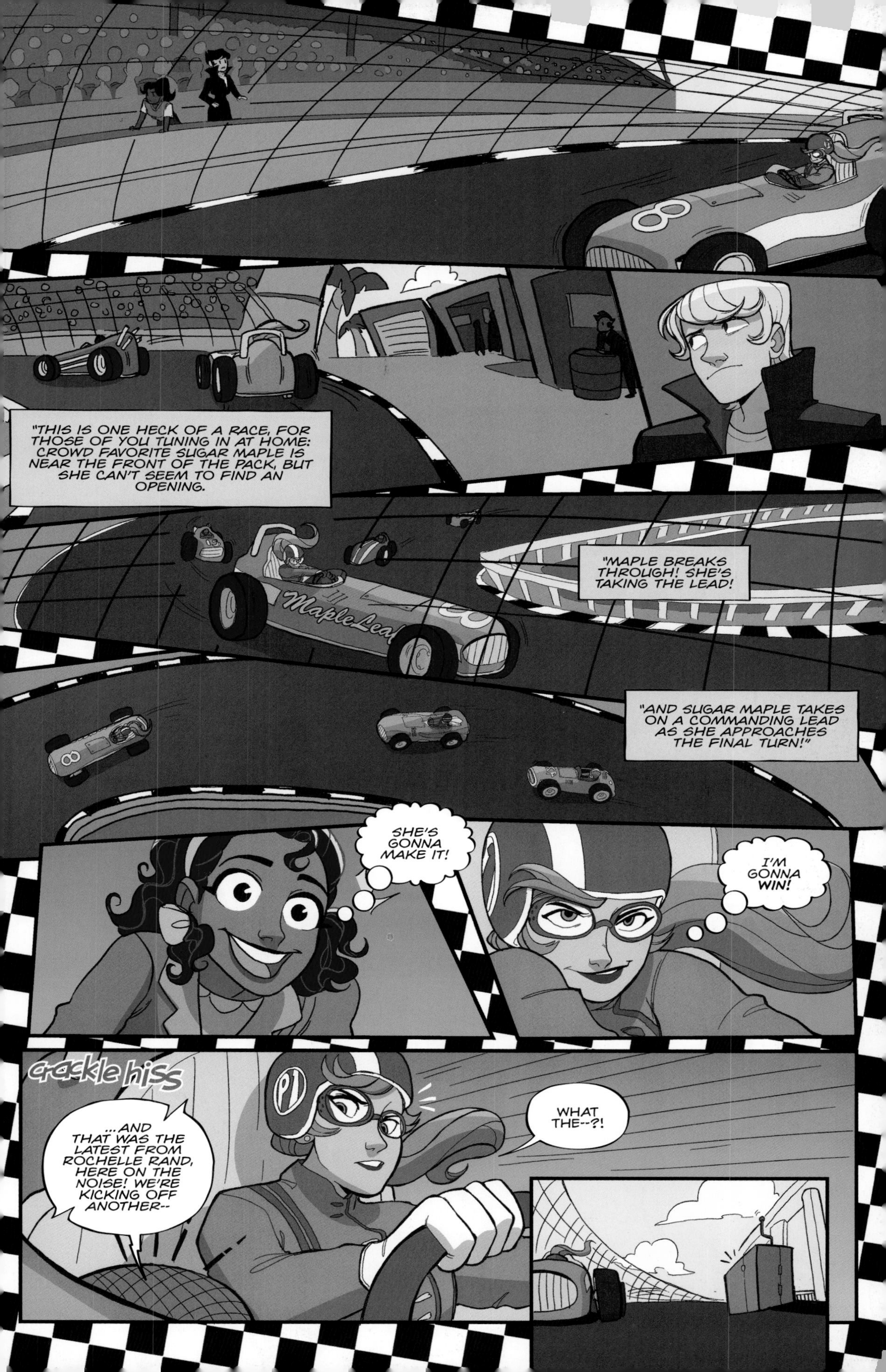
"THIS IS ONE HECK OF A RACE, FOR THOSE OF YOU TUNING IN AT HOME: CROWD FAVORITE SUGAR MAPLE IS NEAR THE FRONT OF THE PACK, BUT SHE CAN'T SEEM TO FIND AN OPENING.
Maple Leaf
"MAPLE BREAKS THROUGH! SHE'S TAKING THE LEAD!
"AND SUGAR MAPLE TAKES ON A COMMANDING LEAD AS SHE APPROACHES THE FINAL TURN!"
SHE'S GONNA MAKE IT!
I'M GONNA WIN!
crackle hiss
...AND THAT WAS THE LATEST FROM ROCHELLE RAND, HERE ON THE NOISE! WE'RE KICKING OFF ANOTHER--
WHAT THE--?!

FWOOOOOM
SCRRRREEEEECH
OHMYGOSH!
FWWWOOOOOM
SUGAR!

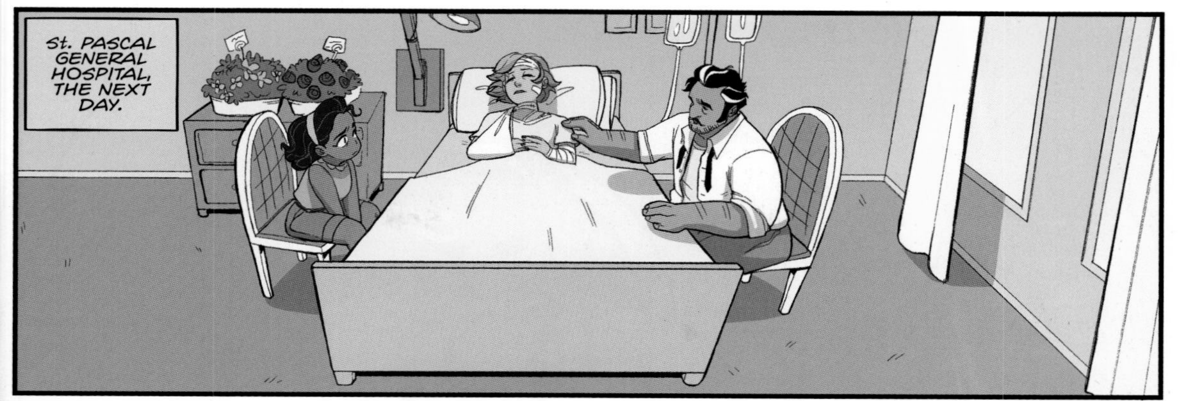
St. PASCAL GENERAL HOSPITAL, THE NEXT DAY.

I KNOW WHAT YOU'RE THINKING, GOLDIE. I COULD'VE STOPPED HER FROM DRIVING.

I'VE NEVER BEEN THE BEST FATHER TO SUGAR. I KNOW THAT...
BUT SHE WAS SO EASY COMPARED TO HER SISTER. AND THEN I JUST GOT SO WRAPPED UP IN THE BUSINESS END OF THINGS... AND SHE SEEMED SO CONTENT WITH PRESENTS. I TOOK HER FOR GRANTED...

SHE'S GOING TO BE ALRIGHT, MR. MAPLE. YOU KNOW, WHEN I WENT THROUGH TOUGH TIMES, MY DAD DIDN'T ALWAYS KNOW WHAT TO SAY. SOMETIMES HE SAID REALLY DUMB STUFF THAT DIDN'T SEEM TO HELP MUCH...

BUT HE ALWAYS LISTENED. HE WAS ALWAYS THERE FOR ME. THAT'S ALL THAT REALLY MATTERED. THAT'S ALL SUGAR WANTS FROM YOU.

I JUST... I CAN'T BELIEVE RED WOULD GO THIS FAR. SHE WAS CRUEL AS A GIRL, BUT I'D HOPED... MOTHERHOOD HAD SOFTENED HER. APPARENTLY NOT. HER POOR GIRLS.
FROM WHAT I HEAR, THEIR FATHER IS EVEN MORE INVOLVED IN HIS CAREER THAN ME. HE'S A RADIO MAN, BUT THAT'S ABOUT ALL I KNOW...

Did... did I win?
SUGAR! SWEETHEART, DON'T YOU REMEMBER?

I REMEMBER... I HEARD ROCHELLE RAND ON THE RADIO.

SUGAR, DARLING, I--I'M SO SORRY.

THIS IS REALLY SWEET, BUT SUGAR'S GONNA FLIP HER WIG WHEN SHE SEES HER NEW HAIRCUT...
07

AND WHAT'S GOING TO HAPPEN TO CROSSED PALMS?

GOLDIE. WE THINK IT'S TIME THAT YOU GO HOME. THE POLICE HAVE PICKED UP THE INVESTIGATION.
BESIDES, YOU'RE TOTALLY CLANKED, YOU NEED SLEEP!

THIS IS THE EXHAUSTION OF BEING SO CLOSE TO THE END OF A CASE.
THIS IS THE COTTON-MOUTH OF TRUTH, CHER! THESE ARE THE EYE-BAGS OF RIGHTEOUSNESS!

I'M ALMOST THERE, I CAN FEEL IT IN MY BONES.
WHAT YOU'RE FEELING ARE SOMATIC SYMPTOMS BROUGHT ON BY PROLONGED SLEEP DEPRIVATION.

LOOK, I APPRECIATE THE CONCERN, BUT I PROMISE, I WILL SLEEP THE SECOND THIS CASE IS SOLVED.
NOW, YOU CAN EITHER GIVE ME A RIDE BACK TO THE TRACK, OR I CAN THUMB IT, IT'S UP TO YOU.

FINE. IN THAT CASE, HERE. WE BROUGHT YOU FOOD.
AND COFFEE.

HAVE I TOLD YOU BOTH LATELY THAT YOU'RE THE TWO MOST WONDERFUL PEOPLE ON THIS ENTIRE PLANET?
Not lately...
LET'S GO. THE SOONER WE GET YOU TO THE TRACK, THE SOONER YOU'LL BE ABLE TO SLEEP.

ST PASCAL SPEEDWAY
"ALRIGHT, AGENT LADNER: WHAT'S THE SCOOP?"
"IT LOOKS LIKE OUR SABOTEUR PLANTED EXPLOSIVES IN THE TRACK ITSELF--
"...AND REMOTELY DETONATED THEM AT THE EXACT MOMENT SUGAR PASSED OVER THEM.
POLICE LINE DO N
"THE BIGGEST PROBLEM WE'RE FACING IS THAT SO FAR NONE OF THE PHYSICAL EVIDENCE POINTS TO RED MAPLE AT ALL."
8

MY PARTNER'S IN TEXAS AS WE SPEAK, BUT HE HASN'T HAD MUCH LUCK WITH RED'S HOUSE.
THEY'RE STILL TRYING TO HUNT DOWN THE REMOTE TRIGGER THAT DETONATED THE DEVICE, BUT THERE'S ALMOST NO CHANCE IT WILL CONNECT BACK TO RED.
AND THERE'S NOTHING ON THE TRANSMITTER. THEY WERE LUCKY TO FIND THAT THING IN THE WRECKAGE.
TRANSMITTER? DIANE!

YOU'VE BEEN STALKING THE RADIO STATION LATELY--
I HAVE AN INTERNSHIP, GOLDIE, IT'S NOT STALKING.
DO YOU HAVE ANY RADIO CONTACTS IN TEXAS? SPECIFICALLY WCRP EL PASO?
WELL, NOT RIGHT OFF THE DOME, BUT IT'S EASY ENOUGH TO CALL THE STATION AND GET THEIR INFO.

RED MAPLE IS VINDICTIVE. SHE WOULD HAVE WANTED TO PULL THE TRIGGER ON SUGAR'S DREAMS HERSELF.
AND WHEN SHE WOKE UP, SUGAR SAID SHE REMEMBERED HEARING ROCHELLE RAND.
WHAT IF IT WAS THE RADIO? RED COULD HAVE USED HER HUSBAND'S RADIO STATION TO TRIGGER THE EXPLOSION HERSELF!

I'VE GOT WRCP EL PASO ON THE PHONE.

THIS IS AGENT LADNER WITH THE FBI.
I'D LIKE YOU TO TAKE A LOOK AT YESTERDAY'S SIGN-INS AND LET ME KNOW IF YOU SEE THE NAME RED MAPLE.
NO, MA'AM.
ARE YOU SURE?

Oh, BUT THERE'S RED DONAHUE, SHE WAS HERE YESTERDAY. I SIGNED HER IN MYSELF!
Oh, COME TO THINK OF IT, I THINK MRS. DONAHUE'S MAIDEN NAME IS MAPLE...
MA'AM, MY PARTNER IS GOING TO BE VISITING YOU THIS AFTERNOON, I'D LIKE TO ASK YOU TO TELL HIM WHAT YOU JUST TOLD ME.

TWO HOURS LATER.
YOU WERE RIGHT, KID! YOU WERE RIGHT ABOUT EVERYTHING.
IT TOOK SOME DOING, BUT THEY GOT INTO THE STATION AND FOUND A HANDFUL OF EQUIPMENT THE STATION MANAGER HAD NEVER SEEN BEFORE.
AND THAT'S ALL ON TOP OF A SIGN-IN SHEET AND FIVE EYEWITNESSES WHO SAY RED DONAHUE WAS VISITING AT THE TIME OF THE EXPLOSION.
WOAH, NO WAY!

YES, WAY! YOU'RE LOOKING AT A DETECTIVE WITH A BRIGHT FUTURE RIGHT THERE.

EXCELLENT WORK, DETECTIVE VANCE--

Huh. WELL, I GUESS IF ANYONE'S EARNED A NAP AROUND HERE IT'S YOU, *huh*?
zzzzz...

SALE
LADIES AND GENTLEMEN, WHAT YOU'RE HEARING IS THE RIVETING REAL-LIFE COURTROOM DRAMA OF THE **DECADE.**

RICH-GIRL GONE ROGUE, **RED DONAHUE** (FORMERLY RED MAPLE): DAUGHTER OF PROPERTY TYCOON GARFIELD MAPLE--

--GOES ON A **SABOTAGE SPREE** THAT CULMINATES IN THE NEAR-FATAL INJURY OF HER OWN SISTER!

HOLLYWOOD ITSELF COULDN'T DREAM UP A MORE SCINTILLATING STORY!
Persons Magazine

AS THE TRIAL OF THE CENTURY WINDS UP, WE TAKE YOU INSIDE THE COURTROOM--

CROSSED PALMS RESORT, ONE SLOW MARCH OF THE JUSTICE SYSTEM LATER...
DID I MISS IT?
Shhh!
--WHERE THE JURY PREPARES TO RENDER THEIR VERDICT.
YOUR HONOR, IN THE CASE OF THE STATE OF FLORIDA V. RED DONAHUE, WE FIND THE DEFENDANT GUILTY.
THIS IS ALL YOUR FAULT, SUGAR!
YOU ALWAYS GOT EVERYTHING, AND YOU NEVER DESERVED ANY OF IT!
DO YOU HEAR ME, SUGAR? ARE YOU LISTENING TO ME?!

tug
Are we going to live with Aunt Sugar, now?
MISS MAPLE, MISS MAPLE! WILL YOU BE ABLE TO CONTINUE RACING WITHOUT YOUR FATHER'S MONEY?
WELL, I'M STILL TOO INJURED TO COMPETE THIS SEASON. BUT, I'M HOPING I'LL BE ABLE TO RACE AGAIN SOON, AS I HAVE MY OWN MONEY NOW.
WHAT DO YOU MEAN, SUGAR?
I JUST STRUCK A DEAL WITH MONUMENTAL PICTURES TO SELL MY LIFE RIGHTS. I FIGURE I MIGHT AS WELL GET SOMETHING OUT OF IT. IT'S NOT THE SAME AS WHAT DADDY USED TO MAKE, BUT IT WAS ENOUGH TO SAVE A COUPLE OF KEY PROPERTIES.

...WELL, MY PERSONAL VOTE IS FOR YVONNE LEROI TO PLAY ME, WHAT DO YOU THINK?
YAAAY!

ALRIGHT, EVERYONE, THAT'S THAT. WE'VE STILL GOT WORK TO DO, THANKS TO MISS MAPLE.

SHE WAS A GOOD SIDEKICK, I SURE HOPE ALL THIS FAME DOESN'T GO TO HER HEAD.
Local Teen Detective Helps Convict Sister Saboteur.

MARIGOLD, IF YOU PLAN TO SPEND YOUR ENTIRE DAY OFF HERE, I'M SURE WE CAN FIND SOMETHING FOR YOU TO DO.
riiiing
CROSSED PALMS, THIS IS CHERYL, HOW CAN I HELP YOU?
JUST A MOMENT, PLEASE.
MR. VANCE, IT'S FOR YOU.
THIS IS ARTHUR VANCE.

MR. MAPLE! GOOD AFTERNOON, SIR.

YES... I UNDERSTAND. I--WHAT?! YES. YES, OF COURSE, SIR! GOOD LUCK TO YOU, SIR.

HE WANTED TO REITERATE TO ME THAT CROSSED PALMS IS SAFE.
AND HE'S ASKED ME TO TAKE ON MORE RESPONSIBILITIES WHEN HE LEAVES FOR CALIFORNIA.
AND THERE'S A RAISE. *Wow, what a raise...*

THAT'S INCREDIBLE, DAD! I KNEW SUGAR'D DO RIGHT BY YOU!
THERE ARE MORE DETAILS TO WORK OUT, BUT... WOW...
YOU KNOW, WHEN WE WERE KIDS I WOULD ***NEVER*** HAVE BELIEVED THERE WAS ANYTHING MORE THAN A SPOILED BRAT UNDERNEATH SUGAR'S PRICKLY PRINCESS EXTERIOR, BUT SHE REALLY CAME THROUGH!
IT'S PRETTY WONDERFUL OF HER TO TAKE HER NIECES ON, TOO.
IS IT JUST ME, OR IS SUGAR GONNA BE THE HIPPEST AUNT ON THE PLANET?

SHE'LL TEACH THEM HOW TO BE FASHIONABLE, AND NOT TO TAKE LIP FROM MEAN BOYS...
SHE'LL BUY THEM FANCY CARS WHEN THEY DO HER A GOOD TURN...
WHAAAAAAAAAT?
WHAAAAAAAT??
WHHAAAAAAAAAAAAAA
--AAAT?
DIANE IS THIS FOR REAL? I'M NOT DREAMING, AM I?
THERE'S A NOTE.
Goldie--
I hope your dad enjoys his promotion. He's always been decent to me, and I wish you hadn't made me so mad at you that I got him fired that one time. Anyway, take care of my car, cause if you hurt her in any way, I'll be in Florida so fast you'll get whiplash. Not a scratch!
Sincerely,
Your sidekick
Sugar Maple

I FORGIVE SUGAR MAPLE FOR EVERY NASTY THING SHE'S EVER SAID TO ME! SHE'S AN ANGEL, SHE'S A WONDER! THEY OUGHTA MAKE HER A SAINT!

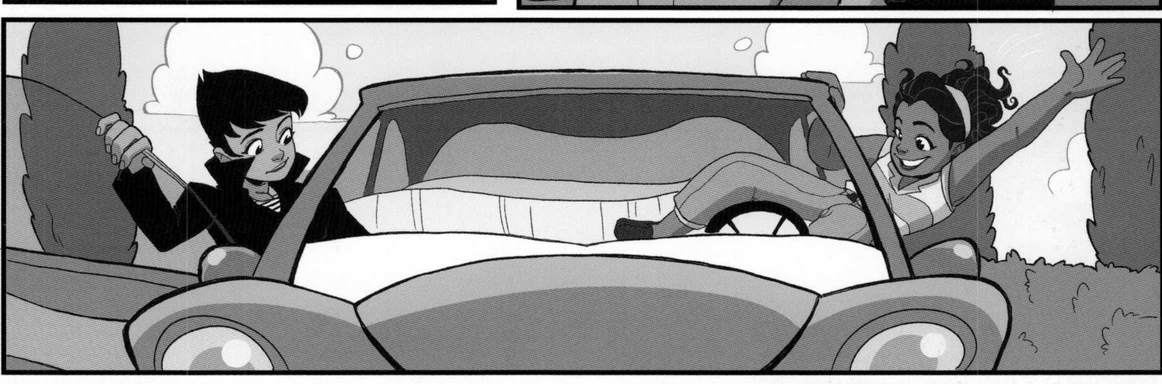

VVVRRRRMMMMMMMM
WHERE SHOULD WE GO? WHERE DO YOU WANT TO GO, DIANE, I CAN TAKE YOU ANYWHERE IN *MY NEW CAR!*
LET'S JUST SEE WHERE THE ROAD TAKES US.
WOOOOOOOOHOOOOOOOOO!

GRRRR...

Local Teen Detective Helps
Convict Sister Saboteur.
GOLDIE!
given about a specific A sister The female
topic. The topic of this sibling, sibling in this instance is people are sisters, and
article is: Sabotage! Red is unusual that two
There was a sabotage a sister named people connected in such
that recently occurred, Donahue. And the person
and if the headline of she was sabotaging was a
to be also a sister. That
The Adventure Continues!

Goldie Vance concept art by **Noah Hayes**

1
2
3
4
5
6

Goldie Vance concept art by **Brittney Williams**

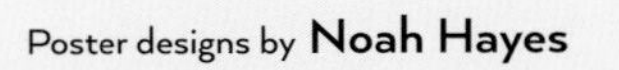

Poster designs by **Noah Hayes**

CASE STUDY
from script to page
8

ISSUE NINE: PAGE TWELVE

PANEL ONE: Goldie and Sugar are in Sugar's Cheetah-Swan.

GOLDIE: All right, Sugar, what gives? Must be the end times if you're asking for my help.

SUGAR: I think someone's trying to sabotage me.

PANEL TWO: Close on Sugar.

SUGAR: My P1 car's been acting…funny. I know that car. Someone's been tampering with it, I'm sure of it.

PANEL THREE: Goldie smirks.

GOLDIE: It's a poor craftswoman that blames her tools, Shug. Sure that P1 isn't more than you can handle?

PANEL FOUR: In the rearview mirror, Sugar's eyes cut to Goldie, glinting angrily.

SUGAR: Really, "Dee?" More than I can handle?!

PANEL FIVE: In silhouette they pull up next to a car at a stoplight.

SUGAR: I'll *show* you what I can handle.

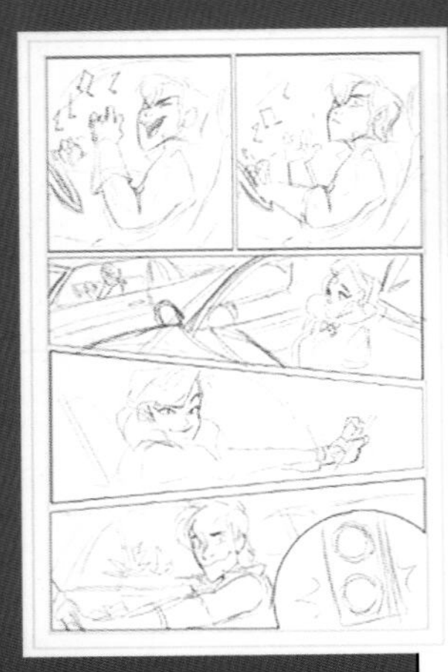

ISSUE NINE: PAGE THIRTEEN

PANEL ONE: Skunk is in his car, singing to himself.

PANEL TWO: There are two short beeps from outside. He glances out the window.

SFX: HONK! HONK!

SKUNK: Huh?

PANEL THREE: He looks up to see the girls in the car next to him, and his eyes almost pop out of his head.

SKUNK (THOUGHT BUBBLE): Whoa! Sugar?! And--that's her! The mystery racer!*

CAPTION: *See Goldie Vance Issue #1!

PANEL FOUR: Sugar revs her engine, eyebrows raised at Skunk.

SFX (ENGINE): vvrrRRM--vrrrRRRRRMMM!!

PANEL FIVE: Skunk looks lovestruck and excited.

SKUNK (THOUGHT BUBBLE): And they wanna race?! Oh man! The guys are never gonna believe this.

PANEL SIX: The light turns green.

SFX (LIGHT CHANGING): Ping!

ISSUE NINE: PAGE FOURTEEN

PANEL ONE: The cars peel out.

SFX: SCREEEEEEEEECH!

PANEL TWO: Both cars zip around a corner.

SFX: VRRRRRRMM!

PANEL THREE: Sugar cuts Skunk off on the next turn, forcing him back.

SFX (SUGAR'S CAR): Block!

PANEL FOUR: Sugar leaves Skunk in the dust. (Skunk likes it.) – inset panel – Chibi Skunk has hearts in his eyes.

SFX (SUGAR'S CAR): VRRRRRRRRRRRRRMMMMMM!

ISSUE NINE: PAGE FIFTEEN

PANEL ONE: Goldie has her head out the window, grinning behind them at Skunk.

GOLDIE: Whoooo!

PANEL TWO: Goldie pulls her head back in, laughing.

GOLDIE: All right, Sugar, I'll hear you out! (continuing)

But only 'cause I respect you as a driver -- not 'cause I don't think you're a she-beast.

SUGAR: Fine.

PANEL THREE: Goldie goes into Girl Detective Mode, taking out her notepad and watching Sugar earnestly.

GOLDIE: What makes you think someone's after you?

PANEL FOUR: Desaturated flashback: Sugar's car crossing the finish line, her

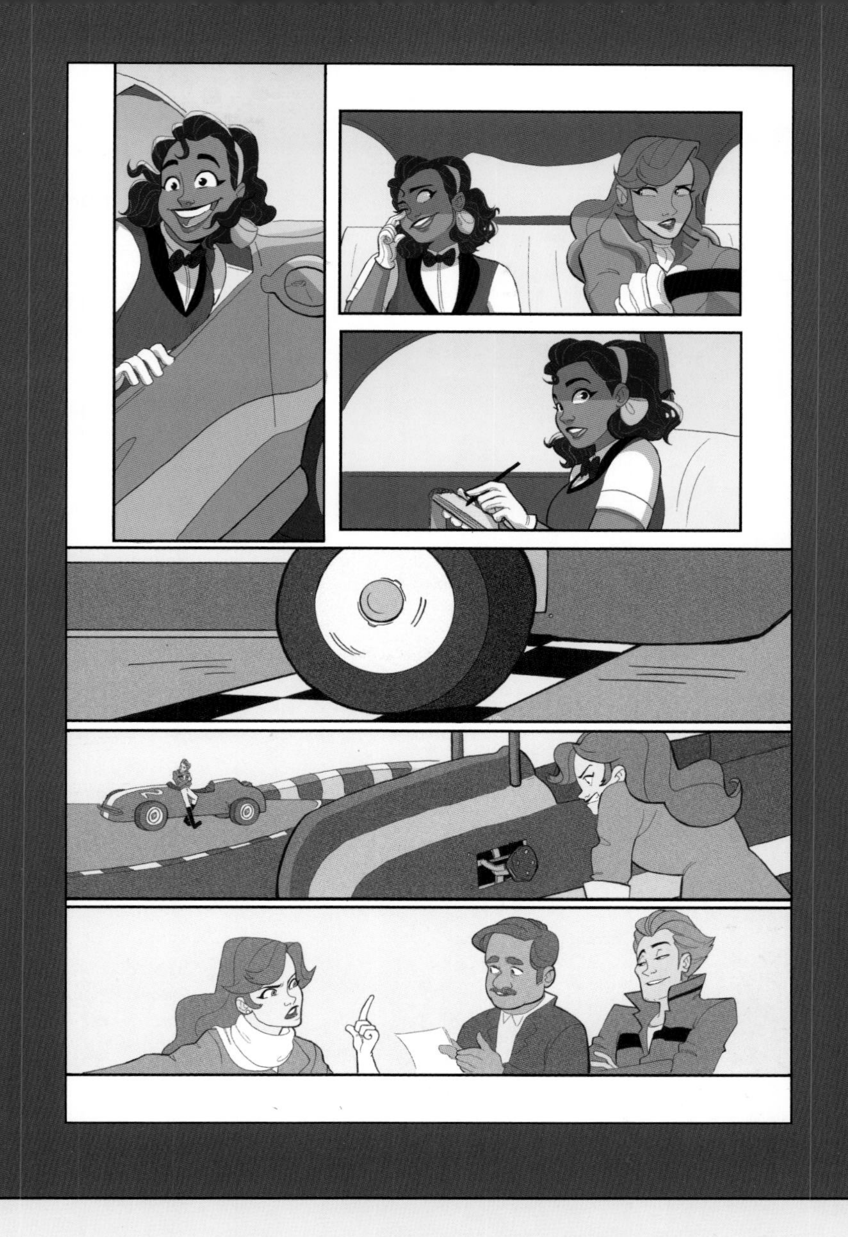

whitewall tires visible. Sugar out of frame:

CAPTION (SUGAR): Usually I race with snowballs, 'cause, well, they look boss.

CAPTION (GOLDIE): Natch. Who doesn't love white-wall tires?

PANEL FIVE: Desaturated flashback: Sugar is unpleasantly surprised to see her tires are gone, and the whitewalls are on Lewis's car.

CAPTION (SUGAR): But last week, that groady weasel Lewis stole them. He took the wheels right off my ride, the night before the race.

PANEL SIX: Desaturated flashback: An outraged Sugar appeals to a racing official who shrugs while looking at a receipt held by a smug and smirking Lewis.

CAPTION (SUGAR): No one believed me. Lewis covered his tracks. He had a receipt for whitewalls, but I'm sure he took mine just to get in my head.

DISCOVER
ALL THE HITS

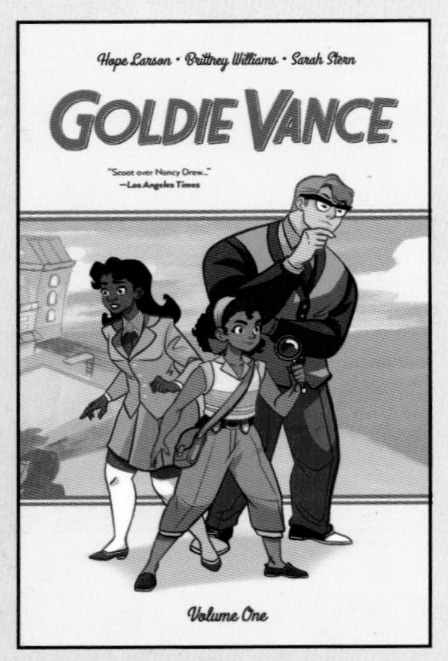

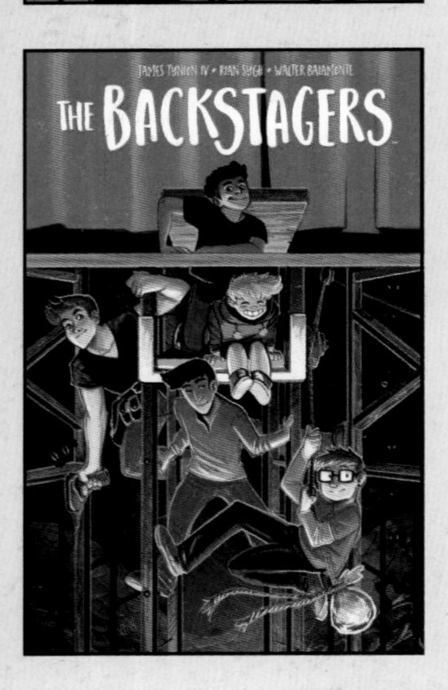

Lumberjanes
Noelle Stevenson, Shannon Watters, Grace Ellis, Brooke Allen, and Others
Volume 1: Beware the Kitten Holy
ISBN: 978-1-60886-687-8 | $14.99 US
Volume 2: Friendship to the Max
ISBN: 978-1-60886-737-0 | $14.99 US
Volume 3: A Terrible Plan
ISBN: 978-1-60886-803-2 | $14.99 US
Volume 4: Out of Time
ISBN: 978-1-60886-860-5 | $14.99 US
Volume 5: Band Together
ISBN: 978-1-60886-919-0 | $14.99 US

Giant Days
John Allison, Lissa Treiman, Max Sarin
Volume 1
ISBN: 978-1-60886-789-9 | $9.99 US
Volume 2
ISBN: 978-1-60886-804-9 | $14.99 US
Volume 3
ISBN: 978-1-60886-851-3 | $14.99 US

Jonesy
Sam Humphries, Caitlin Rose Boyle
Volume 1
ISBN: 978-1-60886-883-4 | $9.99 US
Volume 2
ISBN: 978-1-60886-999-2 | $14.99 US

Slam!
Pamela Ribon, Veronica Fish, Brittany Peer
Volume 1
ISBN: 978-1-68415-004-5 | $14.99 US

Goldie Vance
Hope Larson, Brittney Williams
Volume 1
ISBN: 978-1-60886-898-8 | $9.99 US
Volume 2
ISBN: 978-1-60886-974-9 | $14.99 US

The Backstagers
James Tynion IV, Rian Sygh
Volume 1
ISBN: 978-1-60886-993-0 | $14.99 US

Tyson Hesse's Diesel: Ignition
Tyson Hesse
ISBN: 978-1-60886-907-7 | $14.99 US

Coady & The Creepies
Liz Prince, Amanda Kirk, Hannah Fisher
ISBN: 978-1-68415-029-8 | $14.99 US

BOOM! BOX™

AVAILABLE AT YOUR LOCAL COMICS SHOP AND BOOKSTORE
To find a comics shop in your area, call 1-888-266-4226
WWW.**BOOM-STUDIOS**.COM